# RIP and RAP

written by Amanda White
illustrated by Debbie Harter

## Barefoot Books
*Celebrating Art and Story*

Rip and Rap were twin brothers.

Everyone said they looked
the same as each other.

'No we don't!' Rap said. 'Look!'

He had an extra white stripe on his tail.

Rip and Rap were different on the inside too.

Rap was noisy,

but Rip was quiet.

Rip liked being a sheepdog.
Rap was not so sure.

'I don't want to be
a sheepdog', he said.

And that was
how it started.

Rap went off to play with the piglets.
'What will your Mum say when she sees you?' said Pat the Pig.

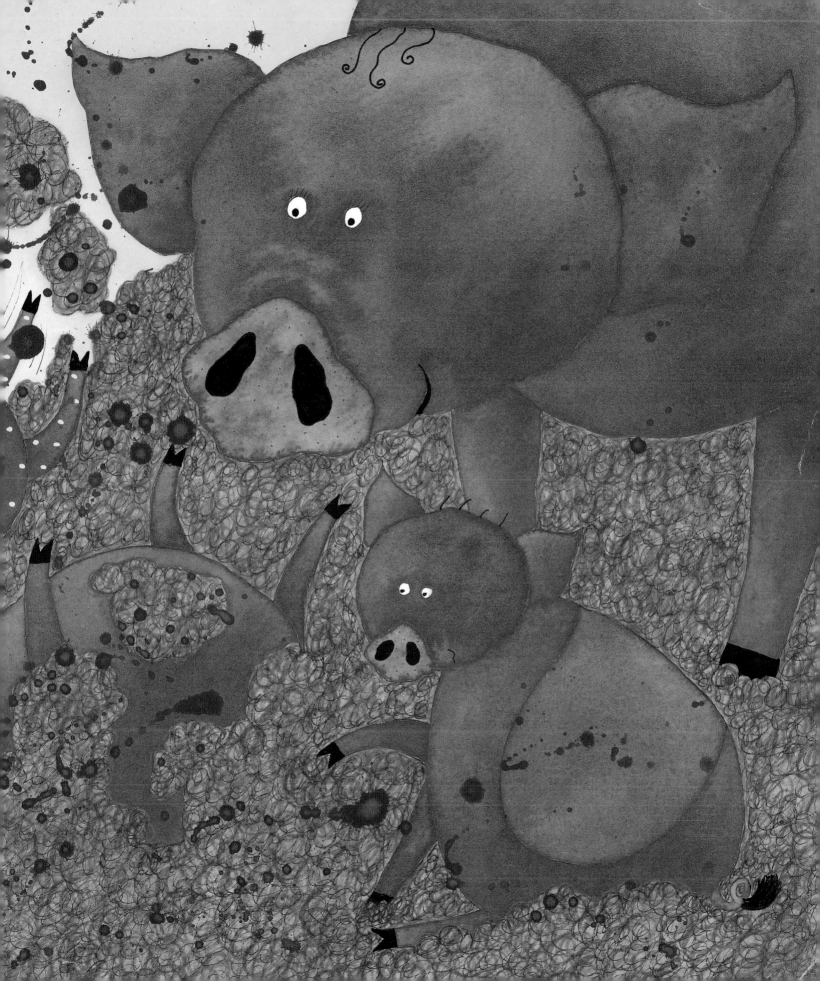

# No one knew who was who.

'Hello Rip and Rip', said Cressida the Cow.

'Hello Rip and Rip', said Dab the Duck.

Rap was so sad that he stopped being noisy.

He went to the back of the barn and hid his face between his paws.

Rip missed Rap.
He had no one to play with.

'Come on, Rap', he said.
'I'll help you.'

They rubbed and scrubbed and
at last the mud came off.

He wagged his tail.

He barked his loudest
BARK!

And Rip and Rap went off together to roll in the long green grass.

For Granda and Mummy — A. W.
For my grandparents, Bertie and Jean Miller Logan — D. H.

Barefoot Books
124 Walcot Street
Bath BA1 5BG

This book was typeset in Providence
The illustrations were prepared in watercolour, pen, ink
and crayon on thick watercolour paper

Graphic design by Louise Millar, London
Colour separation by Grafiscan, Verona
Printed and bound in Singapore by Tien Wah Press Pte Ltd

This book has been printed on 100% acid-free paper

Paperback ISBN 1 84148 993-X

British Cataloguing-in-Publication Data:
a catalogue record for this book
is available from the British Library

1 3 5 7 9 8 6 4 2